An I Can Read Book™

Inspector Hopper

story and pictures by

Doug Cushman

HarperCollinsPublishers

In memory of Arnold Lobel
—D.C.

Inspector Hopper

Library of Congress Cataloging-in-Publication Data
Cushman, Doug.
Inspector Hopper / story and pictures by Doug Cushman. — 1st ed.
p. cm. — (An I can read book)
Summary: Inspector Hopper and his perpetually hungry assistant McBugg solve three mysteries for their insect friends.
ISBN 0-06-028382-3. — ISBN 0-06-028383-1 (lib. bdg.)
[1. Insects—Fiction. 2. Mystery and detective stories.] I. Title. II. Series.
PZ7.C959In 2000 99-30878
[E]—dc21 CIP

1 2 3 4 5 6 7 8 9 10

❖

First Edition
www.harperchildrens.com

Contents

5¢

Ladybug Is Missing

RING!

"Hello! This is Inspector Hopper,

Private Bug, speaking."

"I need your help,"

said Mr. Ladybug.

"Mrs. Ladybug is missing!

I called out 'Ladybug, Ladybug,

fly away home!'

But she did not come home.

I am worried."

"We will be right over,"

said Inspector Hopper.

“We have a case, McBugg,”
said Inspector Hopper.
“I have not had my lunch,”
said McBugg.
“No time!” said Inspector Hopper.
“Let’s go!”

Inspector Hopper and McBugg

arrived at the Ladybug house.

“What is this?”

said Inspector Hopper.

“I don’t know,”

said Mr. Ladybug.

“Mrs. Ladybug was sitting here
eating her lunch.
Suddenly, she was gone!
Only this blue mess was left.”
“This is a real mystery,”
said Inspector Hopper,
“but we will find her.”

"What do we do now?" asked McBugg.

"We will ask around,"

said Inspector Hopper.

"Maybe someone has seen

Mrs. Ladybug."

"Good idea," said McBugg,

"but let's eat first."

"We will eat later,"

said Inspector Hopper.

They came to an apple.

“Hello!” called Inspector Hopper.

“Is anybody home?”

A worm popped out.

“Please be quiet,” she said.

“I just put my baby to sleep.”

"We are looking for Mrs. Ladybug,"

said Inspector Hopper.

"I have not seen her," said the worm.

"I have been home all day."

"Thank you anyway,"

said Inspector Hopper.

Inspector Hopper

hopped through the tall grass.

McBugg followed behind.

"I'm really hungry," said McBugg.

"We will eat soon,"

said Inspector Hopper.

They saw a rat eating a seed.

"Excuse me," said Inspector Hopper.

"We are looking for Mrs. Ladybug.

Have you seen her?"

“Do you think I have time
to look for bugs?” said the rat.
“Go away and leave me alone!”

"What a grumpy rat!"
said Inspector Hopper.
"That seed looked yummy,"
said McBugg.

Inspector Hopper

hopped through the tall grass.

McBugg followed behind.

"I'm really, *really* hungry," he said.

"Okay," said Inspector Hopper.
"We can stop over there
in those blueberry bushes,
but please hurry."

McBugg found a big blueberry.

"Yum!" he said.

"This is very good!"

"Now look at you!"
said Inspector Hopper.
"You are a blue mess."
He looked again.
"It looks just like the mess
at Mr. Ladybug's house," he said.
"I wonder . . ."

Just then they heard a tiny voice.

"Help!" it cried.

"Over there!" said Inspector Hopper.

It was Mrs. Ladybug.

"I came here to get more blueberries," she said.

"I ate too much and rolled over on my back.

I could not get up again."

Inspector Hopper and McBugg
helped Mrs. Ladybug roll over.
"Now fly away home,"
said Inspector Hopper.
"Thank you!" said Mrs. Ladybug.

"Another case closed,"

said Inspector Hopper.

"Yum!" said McBugg.

A

A Boat Disappears

Skeet walked into the office
of Inspector Hopper.
"My boat disappeared," he said.
"That *is* a mystery,"
said Inspector Hopper.
"Tell us what happened."

"I sailed my boat this morning,"
said Skeet.
"Then I went to lunch.
When I came back after lunch,
my boat was gone!"

"What did your boat look like?"

asked Inspector Hopper.

"Here is a picture," said Skeet.

"It looks like a leaf,"

said McBugg.

"It *is* a leaf," said Skeet,

"but it is a good boat."

"We will take your case,"
said Inspector Hopper.
"Show us where your boat was
the last time you saw it.
Let's go, McBugg!"

They all went to the lake.

"Here is where my boat was,"

said Skeet.

“Hmm,” said Inspector Hopper.

“I don’t see any footprints.

But wait!

What is this?”

"It looks like a piece of my boat,"

said Skeet.

"Here is another piece,"

said Inspector Hopper.

"Let's follow this trail."

They followed the trail
of boat pieces.
The trail went past a water spout.
"Hello, Eensy Weensy,"
said Inspector Hopper.
"We are looking for a missing boat."
"What does it look like?"
asked Eensy Weensy.
"Here is a picture," said Skeet.
"It looks like a leaf,"
said Eensy Weensy.
"It *is* a leaf," said Skeet,
"but it is a good boat."

"I have not seen your boat,"
said Eensy Weensy.
"I'm trying to get back up
this water spout.
The rain washed me out."
"Thank you anyway,"
said Inspector Hopper.

Inspector Hopper, McBugg, and Skeet
followed the trail.
"Hello, Sally,"
said Inspector Hopper.
"We are looking for a missing boat.
Here is a picture of it."

“It looks like a leaf,” said Sally.

“It *is* a leaf,” said Skeet,

“but it is a good boat.”

“I have not seen it,”

said Sally.

“I have been jogging all morning.

I have already jogged three feet.”

“Thank you anyway,”

said Inspector Hopper.

Inspector Hopper, McBugg, and Skeet

followed the trail.

"Hello, Conrad," said Inspector Hopper.

"We are looking for a missing boat.

Here is a picture of it."

"I have seen it," said Conrad.

"Hooray!" said Skeet.

"Where is it?"

"I ate it," said Conrad.

"What?" said Skeet.

"You ate my boat?"

"Yes," said Conrad.

"It looked like a leaf.

So I ate it.

I did not know it was your boat."

"What will I do now?" asked Skeet.

Inspector Hopper looked around.
"There are many leaves here,"
he said.
"Perhaps Conrad can help you
pick out a new boat."
"I would be happy to help,"
said Conrad.
"Thank you," said Skeet.
"Maybe you can pick out a boat
that isn't so yummy."
"That is a good idea,"
said Conrad.

"Another mystery solved!"

said Inspector Hopper.

"I wonder what a boat tastes like?"

asked McBugg.

"Let's go home,"

said Inspector Hopper.

Root
Beer

A New Detective

It was night.

Inspector Hopper and McBugg

were walking home.

"I think someone is following us,"

said McBugg.

"It is only our shadows,"

said Inspector Hopper.

"Now someone is above us,"

said McBugg.

"You are right!"

said Inspector Hopper.

"I see their light.

Let's hide behind this shoe."

"Is it still there?" asked McBugg.

"Yes," said Inspector Hopper.

"I still see their light."

"Maybe we can sneak away,"

said McBugg.

"Good idea," said Inspector Hopper.

They crawled slowly
from behind the shoe.
"It is still following us,"
said McBugg.

Inspector Hopper looked up.

"It's the moon!" he said.

"The moon is following us.

I wonder why?"

"Maybe it wants to be a detective,"

said McBugg.

"Of course," said Inspector Hopper.
"Everyone wants to be a detective.
It is a good job."
He called up to the moon.
"If you want to be a detective,
you must learn to follow people
more carefully."

A cloud passed in front of the moon.

"That is much better,"

said Inspector Hopper.

"You are learning fast.

We cannot see you now.

You will soon be

a great detective just like us."

Suddenly, there was a loud CRASH!

“What was that?” asked McBugg.

“It’s too dark to see,”

said Inspector Hopper.

The cloud passed by.

The moon came out.

"Look!" said McBugg.

"A rat is stealing some seeds!"

"Stop!" cried Inspector Hopper.

"You are under arrest!"

"Drat!" said the rat.

He ran away.

"Stop!" cried Inspector Hopper.

The rat ran into an alley.

"Which way did he go?"

asked McBugg.

Another cloud passed
in front of the moon.
Then they heard a THUMP!
"Help!" a voice called out.

“Who said that?” asked McBugg.

“I can’t see,”

said Inspector Hopper.

“It’s too dark.”

The cloud passed by.

The moon came out.

“Look!” said McBugg.

“The rat is caught

in a spider’s web.

He could not see it in the dark.”

“The moon caught the rat,”

said Inspector Hopper.

“It is a very good detective.”

Officer Ant took the rat away.

"Let's go home," said McBugg.

"Being a detective makes me hungry."

"Everything makes you hungry,"

said Inspector Hopper.

And the two detectives walked home
while the new detective
followed them in the sky.

5/00